RICHARD KIDD studied painting at Newcastle University, then took up a scholarship at the British School at Rome. After several years' teaching at Newcastle University he spent a year in San Francisco and six years in New York on a Harkness Fellowship. He has exhibited both in London and San Francisco. Reviewing his first book, *Almost Famous Daisy*, The New York Times Book Review commented that a book such as this 'could persuade youngsters to create their own art - a realization as priceless as anything hanging on the walls of the Louvre'.

LINDSEY KIDD studied fine art at Preston Polytechnic and worked as a mannequin modeller for seven years. She recently started making salt-dough models, including a series of seashore decorations among which was a lobster. It was this lobster that inspired her husband, Richard Kidd, to write *Monsieur Thermidor*.

Richard and Lindsey Kidd live in Warwickshire with their two children.

HOW TO MAKE SALT-DOUGH SHAPES

You will need:

4 tablespoons plain flour • 2 tablespoons salt
½ tablespoon vegetable oil • 4 tablespoons water
+ polyurethane varnish, acrylic paints and brushes

Ask a grown-up to pre-heat the oven to 120°C (250°F, Gas Mark ¼-½) for you.

Mix all the ingredients together thoroughly in a bowl, then knead the dough
for a couple of minutes until it can be moulded easily. Make the dough into shapes.

Again, with the help of a grown-up, put your shapes in the oven to bake until
they are completely hard. This will take several hours, depending how thick
the shapes are. (A 2cm-thick shape takes about 4 hours to dry.)

When the shapes are cool, varnish them with three coats of polyurethane varnish.
Let each coat of varnish dry thoroughly before painting on the next coat.

Colour your models with acrylic paints.

To Lindsey ~ R.K.
To my Mum and Dad ~ L.K.

Monsieur Thermidor copyright © Frances Lincoln Limited 1997
Text and illustrations copyright © Richard and Lindsey Kidd 1997
The right of Richard Kidd and Lindsey Kidd to be identified as the
author and illustrator of this work has been asserted by them in accordance
with the Copyright, Designs and Patents Act, 1988 (United Kingdom).

First published in Great Britain in 1997 by
Frances Lincoln Limited, 4 Torriano Mews
Torriano Avenue, London NW5 2RZ

First paperback edition 1998

British Library Cataloguing in Publication Data
available on request

ISBN 0-7112-1190-6 hardback
ISBN 0-7112-1224-4 paperback

Set in Berling Roman

Printed in Hong Kong

1 3 5 7 9 8 6 4 2

Monsieur Thermidor

A fantastic fishy tale

Richard Kidd

Illustrated by Lindsey Kidd

FRANCES LINCOLN

At the bottom of the deep blue sea there lived a deep blue
lobster called Monsieur Thermidor. He was the proud
owner of the most famous restaurant beneath the waves.

Every evening, sea-creatures swam from fathoms around
to enjoy his famous seaweed soup.

One evening, while the waiters and waitresses
were bustling between the crowded tables, there
was a distant rumbling noise and suddenly…
WHOOOOOSH!…an enormous fishing net swept
through the restaurant, dragging everyone with it.
Up, up it went and landed …THUMMMP! in a
higgledy-piggledy tangle on the deck of a fishing boat.

Next morning, Monsieur Thermidor
awoke with a shiver to find himself lying
on a bed of ice, beneath the striped awning of
a fish stall. His claws were bound with a rubber band
and his view was obscured by a thick hedge of parsley.
"This is a fine kettle of fish!" he muttered.

At that moment, who should be walking through the market but a chef called Henry. He was a kind man and a good cook, but his restaurant was nearly always empty. People seemed to prefer the other restaurants in town.

"This is a fine kettle of fish!" he muttered.

Then he saw Monsieur Thermidor.

"Ahhh, lobster! Now there's an idea. If I put lobster on my menu, perhaps people will want to eat at Chez Henry."

Henry paid the fishmonger, popped Monsieur Thermidor in his shopping bag and cycled off, whistling merrily.

Back in his restaurant, he carefully removed the rubber
bands and lowered Monsieur Thermidor into a tank
of cool sea-water.

By now, Monsieur Thermidor was rather enjoying
this adventure, and he settled down to watch the
comings and goings in the street outside.

That evening, Chez Henry was almost half-full.
Monsieur Thermidor was curious to see what
was drawing them in, so he peered over at a menu.
There, written in large letters, was,

"TONIGHT'S SPECIAL - LOBSTER SOUP".

When Henry came over to the tank for Monsieur Thermidor, he couldn't help noticing the lobster's sad expression.

Henry's heart melted.

"It's no good. I can't cook this lobster. Ladies and gentlemen, lobster is OFF!" announced Henry.

When they heard this, the customers were, too. Soon there was no one left but Henry and Monsieur Thermidor.

Then something strange happened. Tiny bubbles rose from Monsieur Thermidor's mouth and formed words which floated to the surface of the tank:

Henry, you are a good friend.
You have been very kind.
I too am a chef and I would like
to share with you the recipe
for my famous

Seaweed Soup

Bright and early next morning, Henry popped Monsieur
Thermidor into his shopping bag and together they cycled
down to the sea-shore to visit all the best rockpools.
SNIP, SNIP, went Monsieur Thermidor's claws, as he selected
the very tenderest fronds of bubbly black, garish green
and curly crimson seaweed

Back in the kitchen, Monsieur Thermidor
set to work and delicious smells
of cooking began to waft
out into the streets.

Soon, crowds of people
were following their noses to
Chez Henry, where Henry had
thoughtfully decorated the ceiling
with an enormous fishing-net.

By lunchtime, Chez Henry was
the most popular restaurant in town,
and all the other restaurants stood
empty. The other chefs were furious.

Later that night, while Henry lay fast asleep upstairs, there was a CLICK! The restaurant door slowly opened and ten ghostly figures tiptoed across the floor.

Monsieur Thermidor woke with a start. They were after his special recipe!

With a flick of his powerful tail, he leapt out of the tank and snipped the rope suspending the enormous fishing-net from the ceiling. WHOOOSH!...the net swept down and caught the chefs in a higgledy-piggledy tangle on the floor.

When Henry came down next morning,
he could hardly believe his eyes.
   "I must take a photograph of this!"
he cried. POP! went the flash.
   Then Henry unravelled the net
and threw the ten red-faced chefs
out into the street.

Every night after that, Chez Henry was packed with contented customers. Henry was delighted. So was Monsieur Thermidor.

But, as time passed, the smell of the sea made the lobster homesick - or, as lobsters would say, seasick.

Henry decided it was time to take Monsieur Thermidor home. One day, they rowed out to the site of an old shipwreck.

"You'll be safe here," said Henry. "I shall miss you, Monsieur Thermidor, but every night, as I prepare your seaweed soup, I shall think of you. Please accept this gift as a reminder of our time together…"

Monsieur Thermidor bowed, and slipped silently over the side, down, down to the bottom of the deep blue sea.

Before long, sea-creatures were gathering at a new Chez Thermidor restaurant, tucked safely inside the old wreck. Even today, they swim from fathoms around to enjoy its famous seaweed soup. Waiters and waitresses bustle to and fro between the crowded tables, whilst Monsieur Thermidor stands proudly in the kitchen doorway, beneath Henry's photograph of…

A Netful of Chefs!

A Netful of Chefs!

OTHER PICTURE BOOKS IN PAPERBACK FROM FRANCES LINCOLN

ALMOST FAMOUS DAISY
Richard Kidd

"Grand Painting Competition - My Favourite Things" announces the poster, and Daisy decides to enter. But what are her favourite things? She sets off round the world to find out. A globe-trotting story introducing favourite themes by Van Gogh, Monet, Chagall, Gauguin and Jackson Pollock, using reproductions from some of their famous paintings.

Suitable for National Curriculum English - Reading, Key Stage 2
Scottish Guidelines English Language - Reading, Levels B and C
ISBN 0-7112-1070-5   **£4.99**

CAMILLE AND THE SUNFLOWERS
Laurence Anholt

"One day a strange man arrived in Camille's town. He had a straw hat and a yellow beard . . ." The strange man is the artist Vincent van Gogh, seen through the eyes of a young boy entranced by Vincent's painting. An enchanting introduction to the great painter, with reproductions of Van Gogh's work.

Suitable for National Curriculum English - Reading, Key Stages 1 and 2,
Art - Knowledge and Understanding, Key Stage 2
Scottish Guidelines English Language - Reading, Levels A and B
ISBN 0-7112-1050-0   **£4.99**

MY STICKER ART GALLERY - MONET
Carole Armstrong

Solve the clues and fill the empty boxes with 20 reusable stickers of paintings by the great Impressionist artist, Claude Monet. Packed with mini reproductions of his best-loved paintings and fascinating photographs of the artist and his family, this unique book covers everything from Monet's first experiments in open-air painting to the magnificent pictures of his water-lily garden.

Suitable for National Curriculum Art, Key Stage 2
Scottish Guidelines Expressive Arts - Art and Design, Level B
ISBN 0-7112-0962-6   **£5.99**

Frances Lincoln titles are available from all good bookshops.
Prices are correct at time of publication, but may be subject to change.